THE THREE WATER DROP BROTHERS

Written by Lee Eun-hee
Illustrated by Yun Mi-sook
Translated from Korean by Asuka Minamoto

Enchanted Lion Books
NEW YORK

A long, long time ago, planet Earth was born.
Planet Earth was very, very hot.
Lava gushed out of the ground—
here, there, and everywhere—creating vapor.

Since lava is heavy,
it flowed down, down, down.
And since vapor is light,
it floated up, up, up,
turning into clouds in the sky.

The clouds grew bigger and bigger, and it began to rain.
Pitter patter, pitter patter.

Three drops of water fell to the ground.
Splish splash, splish splash.

The rain continued to fall, cooling the hot ground.
Before long, the raindrops came together, forming an ocean.
It was there that the three water drop brothers lived.

As time passed, the ocean began to change.
Soon, green plankton were floating around,
seaweed took root, and coral of every color began to grow.

Trilobites crept across the sea floor, clad in fancy armor.
Ammonites glided past, flaunting their spiral shells.

Then, a fish called the coelacanth appeared.
It was around this time that the brothers grew curious
about the outside world.

The oldest brother, who was very brave,
wanted to go close to the sun.

As he floated up, up, up,
the world became brighter and brighter.

As soon as he reached the sea's surface,
he was bathed in the sun
and felt the warmth of its rays.

One day, he felt himself being lifted
out of the water. He had turned to vapor
and was rising into the sky.

There, the oldest brother, along with many other water drops,
became a cloud.

They were just passing over a mountaintop
when they were shaken by a gust of wind.

As the water drops bumped together,
they merged and grew heavier.
They grew so heavy that they became raindrops
and fell to the ground.

Eventually, it stopped raining.
The cloud was now much smaller and much lighter.
Floating across the sky, the oldest brother traveled
for miles and miles.

BOOM! RUMBLE!

He saw a volcano erupt and watched
as a huge crack appeared in the ground.
He spotted a hungry Triceratops…
and an even hungrier Tyrannosaurus Rex
hiding in the bushes.

The seasons changed, and the world was covered
in snow and ice. The oldest brother was freezing.

Before he knew it, he had turned into a snowflake
and fluttered to the ground.

The snow around him formed a glacier,
and he fell into a deep sleep—so deep
that he didn't notice when the glacier melted,
and he was carried out to sea.

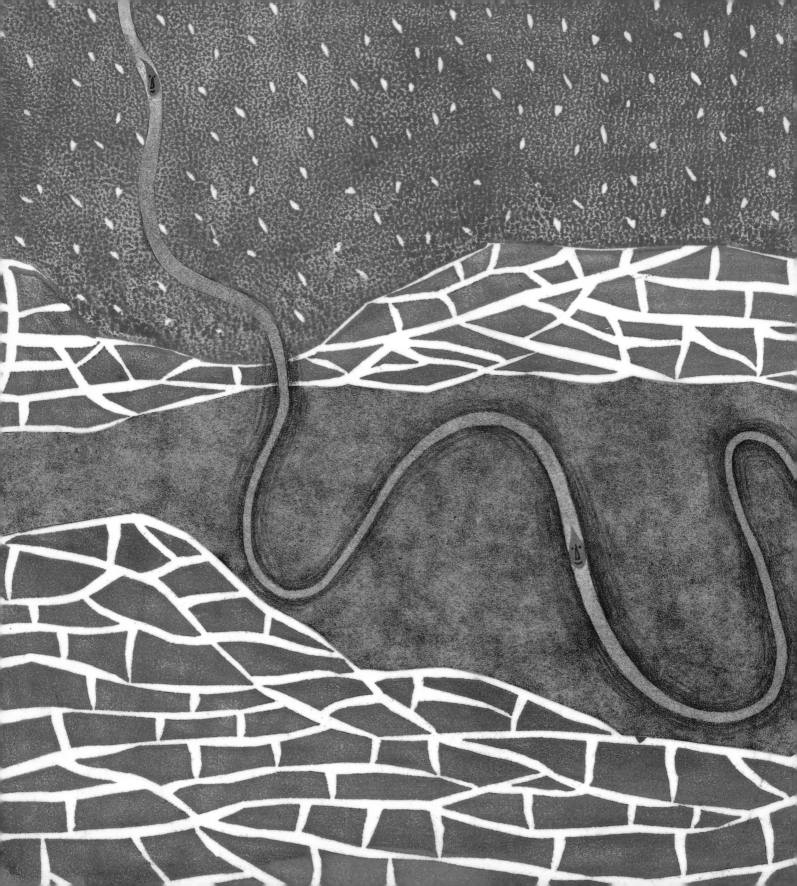

The middle brother, who was very curious,
wondered what life was like underground.
Finding a crack, he wriggled his way in.
Though dark and narrow,
the zigzag path was fun to explore.

Uh-oh! What's this? The path is blocked!
A huge rock is in the way. Are we trapped?

The middle brother didn't give up.
He was determined to find a way out.

But he couldn't do it alone.
One by one, he and his friends
hit against the rock with all their might.
Slowly but surely, they made a hole.

Hooray! They broke through!

The water splashed here and there,
carving an underground cavern with its path.

The middle brother continued on his journey.

The underground world was filled with interesting sights. He saw pitch-black coal
and sparkling jewels; he saw the bones of an animal he had never seen before.

But then, after so much time underground, this brother felt like going somewhere bright.
With the help of his friends, he pushed his way up, up, up towards the surface.

Through a crack between the rocks,
the middle brother flowed into a small spring.
Now he was in a valley, where animals came
to quench their thirst.

Down, down, down along the curving ridge he went.
The farther he went, the more friends he met.
First he was a brook, then a stream, then a river.

He traveled far and wide. *Splash! Whoosh! Splash! Whoosh!*
The ocean came into view.

The youngest brother, who was very shy,
didn't know where to go.
He wandered around for a while,
letting the waves carry him from place to place.

Then one day, a big wave came and carried him
to the top of a hill.
His body seeped into the soft soil,
where grass seeds were just beginning to sprout.

A baby grass shoot reached out its little root,
and the youngest brother got sucked in.
From the root, he passed through the stem,
and ended up inside a leaf.

The leaf had countless green veins
that stretched out in all directions.
With the help of more water drops,
the baby grass shoot grew bigger and bigger
with each passing day.

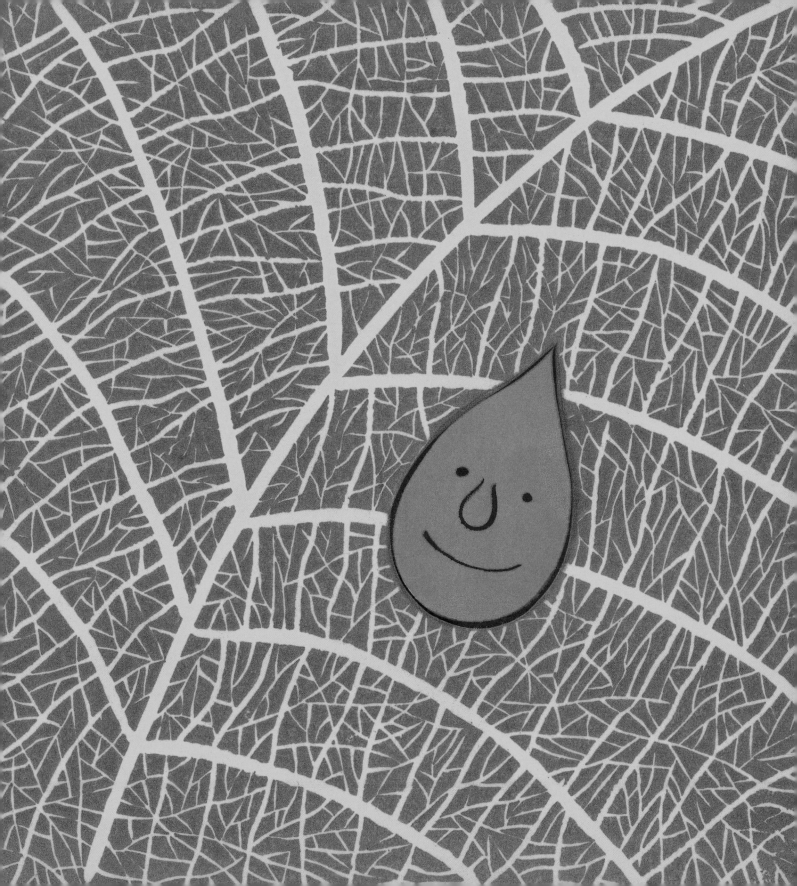

A few days later, a cow came out to the field to graze.
It chewed on the grass and gulped it down.

The youngest brother went inside the cow's body,
passing through its stomach.

He went around and around, around and around,
until finally, he came out as milk.

A little boy drank the milk, and the youngest brother went inside his body. But not for long!

Before he knew it, the youngest brother was swimming in the toilet.

From there, he went on a long, long journey underground.

Finally, he reached the river.
He continued to flow, until he
found himself back in the ocean—
his home.

At long last, the three water drop brothers were back in the ocean, together again.
But their adventures were far from over.
In fact, they had just begun!

Taking different forms and traveling in different ways, they will continue to explore the world.
Because that is exactly what water drops like to do!